In memory of Michael James

SIMON & SCHUSTER BOOKS FOR YOUNG READERS • An imprint of Simon & Schuster Children's Publishing Division • 1230 Avenue of the Americas, New York, New York 10020 • Copyright © 2015 by Carter Goodrich • All rights reserved, including the right of reproduction in whole or in part in any form. • SIMON & SCHUSTER BOOKS FOR YOUNG READERS is a trademark of Simon & Schuster, Inc. • For information about special discounts for bulk purchases, please contact Simon & Schuster Special Sales at 1-866-506-1949 or business@simonandschuster.com. • The Simon & Schuster Speakers Bureau can bring authors to your live event. For more information or to book an event, contact the Simon & Schuster Speakers Bureau at 1-866-248-3049 or visit our website at www.simonspeakers.com. • Book design by Dan Potash • The text for this book is set in 1820 Modern. • The illustrations for this book are rendered in watercolor. • Manufactured in China • 0615 SCP

10 9 8 7 6 5 4 3 2 1

Library of Congress Cataloging-in-Publication Data • Goodrich, Carter, author, illustrator. • We forgot Brock! / Carter Goodrich. — 1st edition. pages cm • Summary: Phillip and Brock are best friends, although everyone else thinks Brock is imaginary, so when Phillip gets tired out at the Big Fair while Brock is still having fun, they are separated and it will take a very special twosome to bring them back together again. • ISBN 978-1-4424-8090-2 (hardcover : alk. paper) — ISBN 978-1-4424-8091-9 (eBook) • [1. Best friends—Fiction. 2. Friendship—Fiction. 3. Imaginary playmates—Fiction. 4. Missing children—Fiction.] I. Title. PZ7.G61447We 2015 • [E]—dc23 • 2014015991

We Forgot Brock!

Carter Goodrich

Simon & Schuster Books for Young Readers
New York   London   Toronto   Sydney   New Delhi

This is Phillip and Brock. They're best friends. They spend all their time goofing around together.

The weird thing is, nobody else can see Brock. Everyone calls him "Phillip's Imaginary Friend." Whatever *that* means.

At dinner, Phillip might say something like,
"Brock would like some more, please!"

But his mom only pretends to give Brock seconds.

Or sometimes, in the driveway, Phillip yells,
"Wait, Dad! Brock has to move his chopper!"

"Please ask Brock to hurry up," Phillip's dad will say.

Brock can also be *really* funny!

But Phillip's parents never get it.

One evening, the whole family piled into the car and headed to the Big Fair.

"Brock wants us to ride the
Brain Shaker!" said Phillip.

"Tell Brock the Brain Shaker is a
big kids' ride," his dad said.

At the Big Fair, Phillip and Brock rode the merry-go-round first. Then the bumper cars. Then the Tilt-A-Whirl.

Phillip got some cotton candy. Brock didn't want any. He only liked beans and spaghetti.

Finally, after the Ferris
wheel, Phillip got sleepy.

But Brock wasn't sleepy at all.
It was time to ride the Brain Shaker.

Phillip woke up as soon as the car pulled into the driveway. "Where's Brock?!" he yelled.

Then he ran inside
to see if maybe Brock
was already home.

But he wasn't.

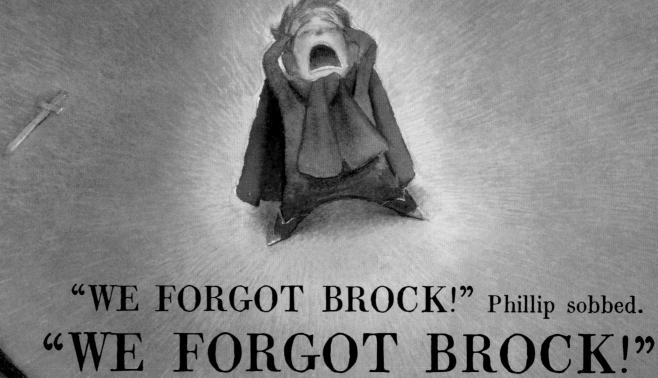

"WE FORGOT BROCK!" Phillip sobbed.
"WE FORGOT BROCK!"

Back at the Big Fair, Brock couldn't find Phillip. He went back on the Ferris wheel for a better view. But he couldn't see Phillip anywhere.

Brock said he was lost, and he wanted to go home.

"My name is Anne," the little girl said. "And this is Princess Sparkle Dust! Would you like to come home with us?"

So Princess Sparkle Dust, Anne, and Brock all went home together.

The next day, Princess Sparkle Dust and
Anne found Brock sitting all by himself.
He missed Phillip very much.

They did magic tricks to cheer him up.

Then the three of them began to invent games and tell each other stories.

Meanwhile, Phillip spent the day looking for Brock.

He searched everywhere, but he couldn't find him.

Just as Brock was beginning to have a lot of fun . . .

he remembered how much he missed Phillip.

And just as Phillip was about to give up his search . . .

"BROCK!!!"

Brock introduced Phillip to his new friends,
Anne and Princess Sparkle Dust.

From then on, Phillip, Brock, Anne, and Princess Sparkle Dust all became best friends. They spent all their time goofing around together.

And everything was even better than before.